THE CARR HOUSE CATS

AT CHRISTMAS

Darien Ross

Illustrations by Avis Rasmussen

Order this book online at www.trafford.com
or email orders@trafford.com

Most Trafford titles are also available at major online book retailers.

Illustrations by Avis Rasmussen B.F.A., M.Ed.

Printed in the United States of America.

ISBN: 978-1-4669-4794-8 (sc)
        978-1-4669-4793-1 (e)

Library of Congress Control Number: 2012920114

Trafford rev. 12/03/2012

 www.trafford.com

North America & international
toll-free: 1 888 232 4444 (USA & Canada)
phone: 250 383 6864 ♦ fax: 812 355 4082

THE CARR HOUSE CATS AT CHRISTMAS

Darien Ross

Illustrations by Avis Rasmussen

It was Christmas and the Carr House Cats were getting ready for a Christmas party with all their friends.

Whiskers was straightening his cuffs.

Misty was tying a tie.

2

Elsewhere, in their own homes, their friends could be found, preparing for the evening.

Lady Pepper was putting on her jewels.   Norris was combing his soft fur.

While Suze dabbed on lavender perfume.   And Percy Peacock was smoothing out

his feathers.

The party was to be held at Emily Carr House. Emily Carr is a well known Canadian artist and writer and her childhood house was now home to Misty and Whiskers.

As they arrived, each of the guests had an offering for the Christmas season. With remarkable pride Misty and Whiskers looked round at all the festive Victorian decorations that filled each room.

Whiskers went up to the tree, his eyes as round as the very ornaments hanging from its branches. He happily tapped a pretty, red bauble with his paw. Christmas was the Carr House Cats' favourite season. They had loved it ever since they were small kittens and the first boxes of decorations were brought out, opened and unpacked. At Christmas time there was always something going on and something to explore.

The Cats loved the fragrant smell of pine that filled the rooms, along with the scent of cinnamon, cranberry and, most importantly, the sweet, sweet smell of the Christmas pudding!

It was always Misty and Whiskers who made the delicious pudding. Their special recipe was made up of all their friends' favourite things. Lady Pepper loved her carrots. Percy Peacock adored his fruit. Norris always had to have raisins and Misty, Whiskers and Suze craved their clotted cream icing. With a big holly sprig in the centre it almost looked too good to eat. But, eat it they would. It was always brought out at the end of their merry evening of fun and friendship. A fitting way to bid each other "Compliments of the Season" and make a Christmas wish.

8

But first, the party must begin. Percy Peacock looked up at the mantle clock and clapped his wings together. "The evening is young, my friends, and there are many things for us to do. Let us start the celebrations." Everyone had an idea on what should be done first. Not knowing where to start, they wrote their ideas down on pieces of paper and drew them from an old bowler hat, so that it was fair to everyone.

The party was now underway. They began by playing twenty questions and then charades; there was much laughter over the funny costumes and masks.

Next came a special performance of the Nutcracker, with Misty in the role of the handsome Prince, Suze as Clara and Whiskers as the evil Rat King.

Wrapping themselves up warmly with scarves and mittens they took the fun outside;

playing in the freshly fallen snow; making snow angels and building a snow kitten.

Trooping back in, noses nippy with cold from the snow, they cozily curled up by the fire. Misty brought each a cup of hot apple cider. With their bellies warm, it was time now to cut into the Christmas pudding.

Whiskers brought out the covered silver tray. All were licking their lips and imagining how good it would taste when the lid was taken off to reveal...

NO CHRISTMAS PUDDING!

It was gone, not even a crumb was left. They all looked at each other and thought, what could have happened to the pudding?

"Someone must have taken it," whispered Whiskers.

"But who?" asked Misty. The Carr House Cats looked round at their guests; each in turn looked at the others.

"It was not I," declared Lady Pepper, "I would never do such a terrible thing."

"Well, no one should be looking at me," pronounced Percy. " Peacocks are proud creatures and we never take anything that isn't ours."

"I may be mischievous but never would I steal," said Norris.

"Don't think I would do it, I am a lady," Suze said.

Misty and Whiskers did not know what to do, they believed their friends and knew that none of those present would have taken the Christmas pudding. And yet, it was gone.

"I think we should search for it!" exclaimed Misty. And so they did. They looked for it in high and low places; they looked for it in the Christmas stockings, under the tree, in fruit bowls and in the oddest of places. But the Christmas pudding could not be found. Misty scratched his head and thought hard about what a cat would do if he was the one to have stolen it? For that is how, understandably, he thought. A cat would be tricky, a cat would be quick and a cat would never tell anyone his trick.

Then an idea came to him, if it could not have been a cat it had to be a creature that tried to be like a cat. Misty knew of only one creature that might try to be like a cat and that was...

Misty whispered to Whiskers, who smiled and nodded, then got down on all fours and began to sniff. It was not the pudding he was sniffing for but the culprit who would be found with the pudding. Whiskers sniffed and sniffed as his friends followed him into the hall, then to the cupboard under the stairs.

He opened the door and who did they find with the pudding in his paws but...

Rochester the Raccoon.

"I knew it was Rochester when I realized that the mystery reminded me of what a cat would do," declared Misty. "Who else, but a raccoon tries to be as swift and mysterious as a cat?"

"But, what I want to know," asked Whiskers, " is why did you take our Christmas pudding, Rochester?"

Rochester bowed his head, "I, too, wanted a piece of the Christmas pudding. It looked so good."

"Why didn't you just ask for a piece of it?" said Suze.

"I didn't think I would be allowed to have a piece, because I was not invited to the party," Rochester said.

"What do you mean not invited? I wrote the invitation myself. I posted it the same day as I did for everyone else. I thought that since you did not reply that you did not want to join us," announced Misty.

"I never received your invitation. Though I did hope and wait for one. It never came, so I thought I was just not invited to the party," sighed a sad looking Rochester.

"The letter must have been lost, for how could we not invite you?" Whiskers asked, patting Rochester on the back.

"We are all very sorry, that you should think that we had forgotten you at Christmas time. We promise that it will never happen again. Would you, please, join us now in the celebration and make a wish on the Christmas pudding?" asked Misty.

Rochester smiled, and thanked them for he would like nothing more than to spend the evening with all of them and to take in the Christmas cheer.

Together carrying the pudding, Misty and Whiskers led Rochester into the dining room. The creatures forgave Rochester for taking the pudding and gave him the honour of cutting the first piece, and together they all made a wish.

Misty and Whiskers then raised their glasses of eggnog and proclaimed,

"Merry Christmas to All and let this be known as a memorable one."

And so it was.

Misty and Whiskers' Recipe for Christmas Pudding

This traditional recipe comes from the author's Great Gramma and would be very much like what Emily Carr and her family ate.

1/2cup soft butter

3/4cup packed brown sugar

1 egg

2tbsp apple juice

1/2 cup each of currents, raisins, dates

1 cup candied fruits

1 cup of flour

1/2 teaspoon of baking soda

1/4 teaspoon salt

1/4 teaspoon of cinnamon

1/8 teaspoon of allspice, ginger, nutmeg

Grease a 5 cup mould or pudding dish and coat with sugar to cover all the bowl. Cream butter and brown sugar together then beat in the egg and liquid. Stir in the fruits. Sift the flour and soda, salt and spices together. Blend into fruit mixture very well. Spoon this into the mould and cover with heavy duty aluminum foil. Sit on a rack in a large pot and add water to halfway up the side of the mould. Cover the pan tightly and steam for four hours. Add water if needed. Store in a cool dry place or fridge. Steam again for an hour and a half before serving.

Misty

Tuxedo cat Misty is our official greeter; often you may find him lounging on the front counter. He loves to be admired and spoken to by the many folk who visit us. At times aloof, Misty can be coaxed to have his photo taken when it suits his fancy.

Whiskers

A little shy but very sweet natured, Whiskers, prefers to be a behind the scenes kind of fellow. He'll peek out from beneath tables and chairs to watch the world go by. Despite his reserve, Whiskers has been known to have a friendly chat with guests.

About the Author

Like Emily and her sisters, Darien Ross and her sister have grown up in Emily Carr House. Darien is inspired by Emily's art, writings and her deep love of animals. Look for more of Darien's Carr House Cats stories in the future.

About the Illustrator

Avis Rasmussen B.F.A., M.Ed., is a painter, printmaker and poet. Her art is widely collected and exhibited. Avis is especially acclaimed for her 'plein air' watercolour landscapes and vignettes.

About Emily Carr and her House

Emily Carr (1871-1945) is renowned as an artist, writer and lover of nature. She was born at 207 Government Street, Victoria, B.C., Canada. Her childhood home is now a National and Provincial Historic Site owned by the people of British Columbia. Emily Carr House is open to visitors from all over the world as an interpretive centre for this fascinating Canadian.

Edwards Brothers Malloy
Oxnard, CA USA
March 20, 2013